A Treasury of
Christmas
Favorites

The Unicorn Publishing House
New Jersey

Twas
the night
before
Christmas

'Twas the night before Christmas,
When all through the house,
Not a creature was stirring, not even a mouse.

The stockings were hung by the chimney with care,
In hopes that St. Nicholas soon would be there.

The children were nestled all snug in their beds,
While visions of sugarplums danced in their heads.

And Mamma in her kerchief, and I in my cap,
Had just settled down for a long winter's nap.
When out on the lawn there arose such a clatter,
I sprang from my bed to see what was the matter.

Away to the window I flew like a flash,
Tore open the shutters and threw up the sash.

The moon on the breast of the new-fallen snow,
Gave a luster of midday to objects below,

When, what to my wondering eyes should appear,
But a miniature sleigh, and eight tiny reindeer,
With a little old driver, so lively and quick,
I knew in a moment it must be St. Nick.

More rapid than eagles his coursers they came,
And he whistled, and shouted, and called them by name:

"Now, Dasher! Now, Dancer! Now, Prancer and Vixen!
On, Comet! On, Cupid! On, Donder and Blitzen!
To the top of the porch! To the top of the wall!
Now, dash away! Dash away! Dash away all!"

As dry leaves that before the wild hurricane fly,
When they meet with an obstacle, mount to the sky,
So up to the housetop the coursers they flew,
With the sleigh full of toys, and St. Nicholas, too.

And then in a twinkling, I heard on the roof
The prancing and pawing of each little hoof.

As I drew in my head, and was turning around,
Down the chimney St. Nicholas came with a bound.

He was dressed all in fur, from his head to his foot,
And his clothes were all tarnished with ashes and soot.
A bundle of toys he had flung on his back,
And he looked like a peddler just opening his pack.

His eyes how they twinkled! His dimples how merry!
His cheeks were like roses, his nose like a cherry.
His droll little mouth was drawn up like a bow,
And the beard on his chin was as white as the snow.

The stump of a pipe he held tight in his teeth,
And the smoke, it encircled his head like a wreath.
He had a broad face and a little round belly.
That shook, when he laughed, like a bowl full of jelly.

He was chubby and plump, a right jolly old elf,
And I laughed when I saw him, in spite of myself.
A wink of his eye and a twist of his head,
Soon gave me to know I had nothing to dread.

He spoke not a word, but went straight to his work,
And filled all the stockings, then turned with a jerk,
And laying his finger aside of his nose,
And giving a nod, up the chimney he rose.

He sprang to his sleigh, to his team gave a whistle,
And away they all flew like the down of a thistle.

But I heard him exclaim as he drove out of sight,
"Happy Christmas to all, and to all a good night."

THE PERFECT TREE

The morning broke late, gray, and cold. If you had the nose for such a thing, you would know that soon it would snow.

Oliver Wendel Badger stood with his nose pressed against the window pane, his furry face framed in a frosty circle. He should be sleeping, he knew, but the older he got, the more difficult it became to sleep through the long, dark, winter—like a sensible badger should.

The streets were filled with noisy cars, and the fields which had been quiet in November were now busy with children out of school for Christmas. Their running feet thudded over Ollie's snowy roof as he tried to snooze beneath the banks of a frozen Mill Creek.

"Impossible," he thought. "Trying to sleep is useless in this noisy place."

Many seasons ago when he had been a small ball of fur, the banks of Mill Creek had been a quiet place—full of new and exciting adventures. His parents had taken him for long, quiet walks through the summer woods hunting berries and luscious roots for dinner.

They would bring these home in a large basket woven from the reeds that grew along the creek, and his mother would make the most delicious wild-root soup and mouth-watering hot berry pie for dessert.

But, those days were gone. Now, Oliver Wendel Badger lived alone—with only his memories of those long-ago walks. His only family now was his close friend, Stanley Livingston Hare, who lived in the woods by Mill Creek with a large family of fieldmice.

Stanley was a crabby old hare, but his conversation was all that Ollie had to keep him company on these sleepless winter days and evenings. And, Stanley made the most delectable crab apple turnovers which he served with piping hot, pine-needle tea.

As always, the thought of Stanley's warm hutch and friendly food made Ollie's mouth water. Perhaps, a mid-winter dinner would be just the thing to calm Ollie's frazzled nerves.

A "holiday feast!" exclaimed Ollie aloud. "Why Hare and I could put together a holiday celebration as if we were family."

"The fieldmice could help. Hare could bake his scrumptious turnovers, the mouse family could make their favorite acorn bread, and I . . ." Ollie stopped there.

"I really can't make anything that would go along with the feast," he thought. "My meager dishes are fit only for dining alone."

Ollie was thoughtful.

To a knowledgeable observer (one who is familiar with the ways of badgers) Ollie's twitching nose meant that he was deep in thought. After some minutes, he sprang from the window and threw on his winter coat.

"I'll bring the tree!" he shouted. "We can't have a proper holiday without a tree—a big, green tree covered with popcorn and wild cranberries and pieces of dried flowers."

A tree, to be sure.

Grabbing his little axe, which he used to gather small twigs for his winter fire, Ollie burst from his small front door beneath the banks of Mill Creek and started off across the snow fields in search of the perfect tree.

As Ollie walked, he sang to himself in his quiet, badger voice, a little Christmas song his mother had taught him many years ago.

O Christmas tree! O Christmas tree!
   How evergreen your branches.
Not only green when summer glows,
   But in the winter when it snows.
O Christmas tree! O Christmas tree!
   How evergreen your branches.

Through the cold morning, Ollie searched for the perfect tree. He searched high and he searched low, but nowhere could he find a tree just right for his needs (that is, a tree small enough for a badger to cut down and carry through the woods to the hutch of Stanley Livingston Hare).

Ollie had just about decided that a party was not such a great idea after all when suddenly he spied, in the distance, the perfect tree.

It was small, about his own height, and it was the greenest tree he had ever seen. Ollie was wild with delight! He ran in his fastest badger fashion to the tree.

"A beautiful tree," he thought, "and a trunk just small enough for my axe."

He dug out the snow around the base. He brushed the ice from his axe. He raised it high in the air above his head. And, then he let it down slowly.

The tree, like Ollie, was small and lonely, but it had grown in this spot for many years. It would be such a shame to cut it now, before it had a chance to grow to the size of the other large trees in the surrounding forest.

It would never know the pleasure of swaying in the summer breeze, of having the company of birds and squirrels who would build homes in its branches. It would never sing, as its brothers and sisters did, with the wind, to the night-time sky.

Oh, it would be bright and gay for a few weeks in the home of Stanley Hare. It would be dressed in holiday colors for a brief time—but, then it would turn brown as it died. Its needles would fall off, and, eventually, it would be cast out into the snow or burned in the hearth, giving its last offering as heat and the sweet smell of a spruce-wood fire.

No, Ollie couldn't do it. But, what about the party? What would a party be without a bright, holiday tree? This was too much to think about for such a small badger. He would go to Stanley's hutch and ask him what to do. Stanley always had an answer, sometimes to questions Ollie hadn't even asked.

"Show me the tree," was Stanley's answer.

He had thought the idea of a party was a fine one. He had agreed to make his famous turnovers and pine-needle tea, and even a holiday punch of melted snow and sweet maple syrup. The fieldmice were already baking acorn bread and were eager to string popcorn and cranberries for the tree.

But Stanley understood Ollie better than anyone, and if the lonely badger saw something special in the little tree, then he must also see it.

So, wrapped against the cold and accompanied by the fieldmouse father, the friends trudged off toward where Ollie's perfect tree grew.

"There it is!" cried Ollie, obviously excited again at the sight of such a perfect tree. And, sure enough, it was. Stanley agreed that it was the finest tree he had ever seen. The fieldmouse father scampered around the trunk in excitement, slipping on the ice and making loud, squeaky noises.

A fine tree indeed—so fine, in fact, that Ollie began to hum again, the song of the Christmas tree.

Soon his quiet hum was joined by Stanley Hare's strong voice; and, before long, the fieldmouse father added his squeaky sounds to the verse.

O Christmas tree! O Christmas tree!
    How evergreen your branches.
Not only green when summer glows,
    But in the winter when it snows.
O Christmas tree! O Christmas tree!
    How evergreen your branches.

The words hung before them like their frosty breath for a moment, then disappeared into the winter air.

"You are right," said Stanley. "We cannot cut such a fine tree, even for our party. We must do without a tree."

Ollie's furry face grew long. "But, I so wanted to bring something to the party," he said. "You are all providing food and cheer, and I have nothing to bring but my hungry self. And what is a holiday party without a tree?"

Stanley thought for a long moment.

The day was rapidly drawing to a close. The moon could now be seen in the still, blue sky, and he knew that night was not far off. Of course, for most wild things, night was a time of activity, but there were still turnovers to bake and punch to make.

"We'll decorate it here," he said. "The fieldmouse family should be finished stringing the popcorn and cranberries by now. We will bring them to the tree and put them on here in the woods."

"What a splendid idea!" cried Ollie. "That way we won't have to cut it down, and we shall have a holiday tree after all!"

And so, in no time at all, they were decorating the small, green tree with all manner of festive dress. The field-mouse family dragged the many ornaments they had made to the tree as Stanley and Ollie hung them on the branches.

The red and white strings of popcorn and cranberries stood out brightly against the dark green branches. It wasn't long before the small tree looked as big as the largest tree in the forest.

They all stood back in wonder to gaze at their fine work.

"There now, isn't that a fine job?" said Stanley Hare.

And indeed it was. A beautifully decorated holiday tree now stood where once was only a lonely little sapling.

"A fine job," murmured the mouse family together.

In the quiet of the moment, Stanley began to sing. It was a song so soft that it seemed to become a part of the dark, quiet forest itself.

Silent night, holy night,
All is calm. All is bright.
'Round yon Virgin, mother and child.
Holy infant, so tender and mild.
Sleep in heavenly peace.
Sleep in heavenly peace.

The friends stood for a while admiring their work, then Stanley said, "We have our tree, but our meal is still to be made, and it is very far from here to my house. We had better be going if we are to have a feast tonight."

Ollie knew that he was right, but he hated to leave his lovely tree so soon.

"But, it doesn't have a star for the top," he said, hoping to delay for just a while longer.

"We have nothing to make a star from, Ollie," said the fieldmouse father. "Besides, we have done enough decorating for one day. It is getting quite cold and our stomachs are hungry for hot acorn bread and crab apple turnovers."

"Quite right," agreed Stanley. "We must be going now."

So together they turned and began the walk back to the hutch of Stanley Livingston Hare where dinner would soon be served to the cold and hungry gathering.

"I am happy," said Ollie, "that we did not cut down the little tree. But, I am sad that I did not get to bring something for our holiday feast."

"But you did," said Stanley. "You brought us a gift we may all cherish, not only now, but the whole year through. You brought us compassion and love for other living things, Ollie. By refusing to cut down the small tree, you showed us that you care for others, for all our friends, no matter how lowly or small. And, because of your gift, the other dwellers of the forest will now be able to enjoy the sight of our perfect tree for years to come. You have brought the true spirit of giving into our lives."

Despite the cold, Ollie felt warm inside.

As they reached the edge of the clearing and were about to pass into the woods toward the house of Stanley Livingston Hare, they turned to have one, last look at their perfect tree.

It still stood, as it would for many years to come, dark green against a fading day, whispering softly in the winter wind.

And, as they watched, the evening star rose behind it and came to rest, for a brief, shining moment, above its crown.

We Wish You a
Merry Christmas

We wish you a Merry Christmas,
We wish you a Merry Christmas,
We wish you a Merry Christmas
    And a Happy New Year!

Good tidings we bring
To you and your kin;
Good tidings for Christmas
And a Happy New Year!

We wish you a Merry Christmas,
We wish you a Merry Christmas,
We wish you a Merry Christmas
    And a Happy New Year!

The Nativity

In those days the kingdom of Judea was under the rule of the Romans. Although the Jewish people had their own laws, they also had to obey the laws of the Romans. The emperor of Rome, Caesar Augustus, decided he wanted a new tax on the people. So he ordered his soldiers to count all the people in the land. Each person was to go to the place of their birth and be counted.

So Joseph and Mary left their home in Nazareth to travel to the town of Bethlehem. Joseph was of the family of King David and Bethlehem was where they had lived. When they arrived, they found the town was full of people who had come before them. Mary's child would be born at any moment, but unhappily, Joseph could find no room at any of the inns.

Finally, a kind-hearted innkeeper who didn't have a room for them in his inn, offered Joseph and Mary a stable where they could at least have shelter for the night.

There Mary gave birth to her son. She wrapped the little baby in swaddling clothes and laid him in a manger where he could sleep.

Nearby, some shepherds were keeping watch over their sheep in the fields. As they looked up, they saw the angel of the Lord coming down to them. The glory of the Lord shone around them, and the shepherds were very afraid.

And the angel said to the trembling shepherds: "Do not fear, for I have come to bring good news to you. This day a Savior has been born to you—the Messiah and Lord. You will find him in Bethlehem, a baby wrapped in swaddling clothes and lying in a manger."

Suddenly, there came the sounds of heavenly voices all around, praising God and saying, "Glory to God in heaven, and peace on earth."

When the angel had gone, the shepherds said to one another: "Let us go to Bethlehem and see this baby the Lord has told us about." They hurried to Bethlehem and found the stable where Mary and Joseph were with the baby.

After they saw the child, they understood, and the shepherds told everyone they saw about the baby and the angel. Returning to their flocks, the shepherds gave thanks and praise to God for all they had seen and heard.

"Glory to God in heaven,
and peace on earth."

A Christmas Carol

Old Scrooge didn't care for anyone or anything ~ except, of course, his money.
He simply hated everything ~ but most of all he hated Christmas. And when someone wished him a 'Merry Christmas,' he would only grumble, then shout:

"Bah, humbug! Bah, humbug, I say!"

Scrooge's Nephew

And when kind souls came to ask for money for the poor and homeless, Scrooge would just shake his head and say:

"Are there no prisons? Are there no workhouses?"

"Yes, of course," they would say, "but Mr. Scrooge, it's Christmas!"

"Nonsense! I'll have none of it, do you hear? Now leave me alone. I have work to do!"

Mister Scrooge

The night before Christmas Mr. Scrooge was home alone. But he wasn't alone for long. The sounds of clanking, banging, and moaning rose up through the house.

"What's all that noise about? Can't one eat in peace? Go away! Go away, I say!"

But it didn't.

"Ebenezer, Ebenezer Scrooo-oooge!" a voice cried out, and then a ghost appeared, covered in chains, locks, and cashboxes.

"Marley, my old friend, is that you? . . . Why do you want to haunt me?" said Scrooge, shaking with fright.

"I have come to save you from yourself, Ebenezer!" the ghost cried. "Three Spirits shall visit you this night ~ Three Spirits who will show you the *true* meaning and blessing of Christmas! Beware!" And the ghost vanished.

Marley's Ghost

"Humbug!" said Scrooge. "Ghosts and spirits indeed! Nonsense! I've simply had something bad to eat. A bit of bad cheese, perhaps. That's it. I will be fine in the morning." And Scrooge went off to bed.

"Ding, dong!" the clock tolled one, and the first of the three spirits appeared.

"Ebenezer Scrooge," a soft voice called. "Awake!"

"Who, or *what* are you?" cried the trembling Scrooge.

"I am the Ghost of Christmas Past," said the Spirit. "Come, I have much to show you this night."

"I'd rather not. Thank you, just the same. You see, I need my sleep and I've eaten some bad cheese and uh . . ."

"Come!"

Christmas Past

"Where are we, Spirit? This is not my room."

"Don't you know?" said the Spirit. "Have you forgotten your childhood, Ebenezer?"

"Why, this is my old schoolhouse," Scrooge said, "and the child there, can that *really* be me?"

"Yes, Ebenezer. That lonely little child is you. You spent many a Christmas alone. Without friends. Without family. Ah, you were an unhappy boy!" Scrooge broke and wept.

As Scrooge wept, the sounds of music and laughter began to fill his ears. He looked up to find himself at a grand Christmas party.

"Fezziwig! My old boss!" Scrooge cried with joy.

"Yes," said the Spirit. "He was one that *truly* understood the joy of Christmas. Why did you not learn from him?"

Mister Scrooge

"Money-that became your only joy," said the Spirit. "And your only love, Ebenezer."

And Scrooge saw himself young and strong again. And beside him was . . .

"Belle," Scrooge said with a sigh. "I had almost forgotten how beautiful she was."

"You were to marry her, remember?" the Spirit said. "But gold was more important to you, Ebenezer. Look now at the tear-filled eyes you turned away from so long ago."

"No! No! Spirit, take me away! Forgive me, Belle, forgive," and Scrooge hid his face in his hands. When he looked up again, the Spirit was gone, and he found himself back in his room.

Christmas Past

"I must hide! Oh dear, before the next ghost comes!"

"Ebenezer! Ebenezer Scrooge!" a thunderous voice called.

"Ah!" cried Scrooge, as he turned to see a beautiful Spirit sitting upon a feast of food, gold, and presents.

"Come closer, and know me better, man!" the spirit roared. "I am the Ghost of Christmas Present. You have never seen the like of me before!"

"Never!" Scrooge cried.

"Touch my robe, then, that you may learn of me."

"Spirit, take me where you will. I am *beginning* to see I have a great deal to learn this night!"

Christmas Present

"Who's little house is this?" Scrooge asked.

"Why, this is the house of your clerk, Bob Cratchit."

"Bob Cratchit? Why am I here, Spirit?" In reply, the Spirit simply pointed to the door. There in the doorway was Bob Cratchit with his son, Tiny Tim, high upon his shoulder.

"Merry Christmas!" Bob called to his family.

"And a 'Merry Christmas' to you, Bob Cratchit," his wife said, giving him a hug. "And how did our Tiny Tim behave in church today?"

"A perfect angel, my dear, a perfect angel," Bob said. "You know, I believe he's getting stronger every day."

"Yes, of course he is," Mrs. Cratchit said, holding back a tear as she watched her little Tim hobble over to his stool.

Bob Cratchit

"I didn't know of the sick child," Scrooge said.

"Would you have cared if you did, Ebenezer?" the Spirit asked. Scrooge hung his head in shame.

"A toast!" Bob Cratchit cried, as the family gathered round. "To Mr. Scrooge. The Founder of the Feast."

"The Founder of the Feast, indeed!" his wife cried. "That old Skinflint cares not one bit for you or for Christmas!"

"Please, my dear, it's Christmas," he begged. "Now, a Merry Christmas to us all, my dears. God bless us!" And the family all joined in.

"God bless us every one!" said Tiny Tim, the last of all.

"Spirit," said Scrooge, "tell me if Tiny Tim will live."

"I see an empty stool and a crutch carefully preserved in one corner. If these shadows remain unchanged, the child will die."

Tiny Tim

"No, kind Spirit," Scrooge begged, "don't let the boy die."

"It is not by my kindness that he would live, but by yours, Ebenezer. If you *truly* care. Come now, I have more to show you."

Scrooge suddenly found himself at his nephew's Christmas party. The party he had said "humbug" to, when the happy youth had tried so hard to invite him.

"Uncle said that Christmas was a *humbug,* as I live!" Scrooge's nephew cried. "And he believed it too!" Everyone at the party broke out laughing.

"Well, a Merry Christmas and a Happy New Year to the old man, though I doubt he'll have either. To Uncle Scrooge!" the nephew cried, raising his glass in a toast.

"He's a good lad, my nephew!" Scrooge said with affection. "And I . . . I never told him so. Oh, what a fool I am!"

Scrooge's Nephew

Scrooge and the Spirit traveled to many homes, both of the rich and of the poor, to see the love and joy that the Christmas Spirit brought to every home that knew Him.

"My time is almost done," the Spirit said.

"Please, tell me Spirit, before you leave, what is that I see moving beneath your robe?" And the Spirit opened his robe to reveal two small children, clinging to his legs. There was a boy and a girl. Both were ragged, wolfish, and scowling.

"Spirit! Are they yours?"

"They are Man's," the Spirit said sadly. "This boy is *Ignorance*. This girl is *Want*. Beware them both, but most of all beware this boy."

"Have they no place to turn, no hope?" Scrooge cried.

"Are there no prisons? No workhouses?" the Spirit said, mocking Scrooge with his own words. Then he was gone.

Christmas Present

Scrooge stood trembling in the new-fallen snow. He shivered even more when he remembered what old Marley had said: Three Spirits would visit this night ~ Three. Scrooge turned to look about him, and . . .

"Oh, no!" cried Scrooge, and he fell on one knee before a dark and gloomy Spirit.

"Are you the Ghost of Christmas Yet to Come?" Scrooge asked. But the Spirit said nothing, only nodding in reply. "Ghost of the Future!" Scrooge cried, "I fear you more than any Spirit I have seen. Will you not speak to me?"

But the Spirit again said nothing. It fixed its ghostly eyes upon Scrooge, then pointed a bony finger toward the mist.

"Very well, Spirit," moaned Scrooge. "Lead on. Lead on!"

Christmas Future

"And now undo *my* bundle, Joe," said a raggedy old woman.

"I hope he didn't die of anything catching? Eh?" said the fat merchant, with a chuckle. "Now, what do we have here? What? His Bed Curtains! Lucy, you didn't take these, rings and all, with him lying there?"

"Oh, that I did!" said the old woman. "And his good shirt too! Why, they were going to bury him in it! Such a waste! What will you give for the lot, Joe?"

"Don't worry, Lucy," the merchant said. "I'll give you a fair price. Why, the old man had more friends in death than he ever had in life, eh?" And they all broke out laughing.

"Dark Spirit," Scrooge said, "are those my things lying there? Am I the unhappy soul who has died friendless?"

But the Spirit said nothing.

Mister Scrooge

Scrooge had only to blink when next he saw what he dreaded most: the empty stool and the little crutch of Tiny Tim.

"Oh, no, Spirit, no," Scrooge cried. "Tell me it isn't so! Not Tiny Tim! He is so young ~ so kind a soul!"

But *again* the Spirit said nothing.

Scrooge began to weep. When he raised his head, he found he was in a graveyard. The Spirit pointed to a tombstone.

Tiny Tim

"Tell me, Spirit: are these the shadows of things that Will be, or are they shadows of things that May be, only?"

Still the Spirit pointed to the stone. Scrooge drew close. There on the headstone read, *EBENEZER SCROOGE*.

"No, Spirit! I am changed! I *will* be a better man! Please! No, no, no!" And Scrooge woke suddenly to find he was in his own bed! And it was Christmas! The Spirits had done their work all in one night! Scrooge ran out into the street in his bedclothes, crying:

"It's Christmas! Merry Christmas!" Then, spotting a boy who was passing by, he called: "Boy! Hurry! Go down the street and buy the big turkey that hangs in the butcher's shop!"

"The one as *big* as me?!"

"Yes, yes, my lad. What a delightful boy! Heh, heh! Oh, bless you Spirits, bless you! Merry, merry Christmas!"

Mister Scrooge

Scrooge had the turkey sent to Bob Cratchit, and then dressed for his nephew's party.

His nephew was overjoyed when his uncle arrived.

"I've been a fool, my boy," Scrooge said. "Will you still have an old man at your wonderful party?"

And his nephew hugged him, and said: "A Merry Christmas to you, Uncle, a very Merry Christmas, indeed."

And Uncle Scrooge danced the day away with his lovely niece. Why, he was the life of the party!

Scrooge's Nephew

And Scrooge proved he was better than his word. He did many good deeds, and to Tiny Tim, who did NOT die, he was a second father.

Scrooge never saw the Spirits again, but it was always said of him, that he knew how to bring the joy of Christmas better than any man alive.

May that *truly* be said of us, and all of us! And so, as Tiny Tim said:

~ GOD BLESS US, EVERY ONE! ~

Tiny Tim